doughnut
butterfly
fly
bee
daisy
buttercup
caterpillar

To the three women who share my Emily passion:
daughter Heidi, granddaughter Maddison, and editor Christy Ottaviano;
and with thanks to Jane Wald of the Emily Dickinson Museum,
who read my manuscript and gave me (as always) astute comments
—J. Y.

For my dear Judy Sue, who made me discover Emily Dickinson
—C. D.

Henry Holt and Company, *Publishers since 1866*
Henry Holt® is a registered trademark of Macmillan Publishing Group, LLC
120 Broadway, New York, NY 10271 • mackids.com



Photo on p. 34 credited to: O.A. Bullard, The Dickinson Children, oil on canvas, ca. 1840. Dickinson Collection, Houghton Library, Harvard University. Gift of Gilbert H. Montague, 1950.

Library of Congress Cataloging-in-Publication Data
Names: Yolen, Jane, author. | Davenier, Christine, illustrator.
Title: Emily writes : Emily Dickinson and her poetic beginnings / Jane Yolen; illustrated by Christine Davenier.
Description: First edition. | New York : Christy Ottaviano Books, Henry Holt and Company, 2020. | Summary: In Amherst, Massachusetts, in spring, 1834, young Emily Dickinson uses scraps of paper and a pencil nub to write a poem, before she even knows her ABCs, and shares it with her household and garden. Includes author's note about Dickinson's life and work. | Includes bibliographical references.
Identifiers: LCCN 2019018532 | ISBN 978-1-250-12808-9 (hardcover : alk. paper)
Subjects: LCSH: Dickinson, Emily, 1830-1886—Childhood and youth—Juvenile fiction. | CYAC: Dickinson, Emily, 1830-1886—Childhood and youth—Fiction. | Family life—Massachusetts—Amherst—Fiction. | Authorship—Fiction. | Poetry—Fiction. | Amherst (Mass.)—History—19th century—Fiction.
Classification: LCC PZ7.Y78 Em 2020 | DDC [E]—dc23
LC record available at https://lccn.loc.gov/2019018532

Our books may be purchased in bulk for promotional, educational, or business use.
Please contact your local bookseller or the Macmillan Corporate and Premium Sales Department at (800) 221-7945 ext. 5442 or by email at MacmillanSpecialMarkets@macmillan.com.

First edition, 2020 / Design by Mallory Grigg
The artist used Ecoline and Colorex ink on keacolor paper to create the artwork for this book.
Printed in China by Toppan Leefung Printing Ltd., Dongguan City, Guangdong Province
10 9 8 7 6 5 4 3 2 1

# Emily Writes

## Emily Dickinson and Her Poetic Beginnings

JANE YOLEN

Illustrated by

CHRISTINE DAVENIER

Christy Ottaviano Books

Henry Holt and Company • New York

SPRING 1834, AMHERST, MASSACHUSETTS

Little Emily tiptoes into Father's study,
being as quiet as dust.

She discovers a scrap of paper
under Father's desk,
some chance slip.
It is the back of one of his legal letters,
discarded, for he is done with it.

She finds a gnawed pencil stub, too,
on the floor near the basket.

Perhaps, she thinks, I will make a poem.
Her brother, Austin, knows a lot of poems.

She finds yet another piece of paper,
this time in the basket.
She likes it even better than the first,
for it has numbers on it.

Checking to see if Father notices,
she picks that paper out, turning it around
until it fits neatly under her hand.

She scribbles curlicues
and circles,
though not actual letters,
some round like the moon
or a summer peach,
some the spiral of a hanging vine.

A year and a half older,
Austin already knows
how to write his ABCs.
He has tried to teach Emily
to write her name.

"EMILY begins with an E," he says,
drawing the capital *E,*
strict as a ruler,
down the left side of the page.

Emily's lines are never so straight.
She prefers the bend, the curve.

"See, Father," Emily says
to the stern-faced man
busy at his desk,
"I wrote this poem for you."
He nods but does not stop working
nor does he smile.

He only reads on Sunday, Emily thinks.
She likes the Bible stories he reads aloud,
though she does not like sitting still
just to hear a tale.

Sometimes, she thinks, Father is as far away as an island.
There is an island in the Connecticut River.
That is certainly far away.

Emily takes her sheet of paper with its poem
into the bustling kitchen.
“I wrote a poem,” she says.
Mrs. Mack studies the paper with great care.
“What does it say?” she asks.
“I don’t have my glasses.”
Emily giggles and points.
The glasses are on the top of Mrs. Mack’s head.
“Oh, those aren’t my poetry glasses,” says Mrs. Mack.
“Those are my cooking glasses.”

Emily points to the squiggle
on the page. She likes poems,
especially the verses Austin recites.

She reads her poem to Mrs. Mack.
It is a three-word poem.
"Frog and bog!" she says. "It rhymes."

"So it does," replies Mrs. Mack.
"Frog and bog. A very good rhyme indeed."
Then surprisingly she adds,
"*Mee-deep*!" and makes a bullfrog face.

Emily thinks Mrs. Mack's face
looks as if it has turned green.
She certainly sounds like the big bullfrog
that sings at the garden's end.

They both laugh
and share the crumbles
of last night's coconut cake.
Then Emily clears the table
and sets the two small plates
by the side of the sink.

Now Emily climbs the stairs
to find Mother lying in her bed,
a cooling cloth on her forehead.
She often spends the afternoons this way.

“I wrote a poem,” Emily says.
“Frog and bog.”
Mother does not open her eyes.
“Yes, dear,” she says.

"*Mee-deep,*" replies Emily.
"Not so loud," says Mother.
"You will wake Lavinia."

Emily tippy-toes over to the baby's cot,
whispers, "Frog and bog."
Little Vinnie smiles in her sleep.
She always smiles, Emily thinks.
She is even. Just like Austin's straight line.

Vinnie puts her thumb in her mouth,
as if it's a stopper in a bottle.

"Frog and bog," Emily repeats,
licking each word.
They taste as sweet as the honey
the bee bears away.
The frog poem sounds even better this time.

Then Emily goes downstairs quietly
so as not to annoy Mother,
who makes her feel rainy.

Out she heads into the spring garden,
for she has not told her poem to the flowers yet.
There are roses still curled in their buds,
seas of daffodils,
small presents of crocuses.
Emily smiles.
The garden makes her feel all sunny,
like a poet.
"Frog and bog," she whispers,
and thinks she hears in return
the long sigh of the frog.

She puts the poem under a rock
and goes looking for the *real* frog
she heard in the night.
There is no bog in Amherst,
but there are plenty of springs.

She thinks about the real and the unreal.
Perhaps poems are the in-between,
just as she is in between Austin and Vinnie.

Then she goes back into the house
and finds another chance slip.
This one is an envelope
with writing on it.

When she carefully opens it,
lifting the flap,
it looks just like a house.
"Envelope," she says out loud.
She tries to think what rhymes with it,
and cannot.

Mrs. Mack is still in the kitchen,
so Emily goes in to ask.
She holds up the envelope
and says, "What rhymes with this?"

Mrs. Mack takes the envelope
and places it next to her ear
as if she is listening
to what the paper has to tell her.

At last she says, "*Hope,* my dear girl.
That's the best rhyme for *envelope*.
Though in a pinch you might try *cope* or *lope*.
Or perhaps . . . *soap*.
But what you shall make of all those rhymes,
I haven't any idea."

Then they sit down to share
a fresh-baked doughnut.
"Hope," says Emily a bit dreamily
as she bites into her bit.
"Yum!" she mumbles. "I had hoped for that."
The doughnut is as warm and sweet
in her mouth as any new poem.
And as true.

# AUTHOR'S NOTE

It will take forty more years and many chance slips before Emily Dickinson actually writes the envelope poem. That poem was written on a cut-apart and opened-up envelope. She turned the paper until the point of the flap at the top looked like the attic of a house a child might draw. Her pencil scratched words into the peak: "The way hope builds his house . . ."

In her lifetime, Emily Dickinson had fewer than a dozen poems published; most of the rest she sent to family and friends. Today, more than a hundred years after her death, she is America's most famous female poet, and her poems are known throughout the world. There have been plays and movies about her life, and her poems have been set to music and put into well-illustrated books.

As she grew older, Emily would take long walks with her big Newfoundland dog, Carlo, who she called her "shaggy ally." Every once in a while, she would stop and take out some pieces of paper from her pocket—old bills, bits of stationery pinned together, invitations, brown paper bags. Anything would do. And then she'd begin to scribble. Not curlicues and circles. Instead she scribbled words, lines, whole poems. She wrote some of these poems on the back side of a *Chocolat Menier* wrapper, bargain flyers from a drugstore, a recipe for "Kate's Doughnuts." Whole verses set down on a program for a musical event, a discarded draft of a legal note from her father's office.

The middle child of three, Emily lived from 1830 to 1886, most of that time in the Homestead, the Dickinson house in Amherst, Massachusetts. She never married. When she died at age fifty-five, her sister, Lavinia, found nearly eighteen hundred poems hidden away in drawers and trunks. Even more were found later, poems she had mailed to special friends, often within the body of a letter. These included poems sent to her brother's wife, Susan, who lived next door—or, as Emily wrote, "a hedge away."

*Emily, Austin, and Lavinia Dickinson*

With the enormous help of Austin's good friend Mabel Loomis Todd, and later with Austin's wife, Susan Dickinson, Lavinia managed to get volumes of Emily's work published. After Vinnie died, Austin and Susan's daughter, Martha, took on the task of making certain Emily's work was properly seen by the world.

We know very little about Emily as a child. She was clearly bright and loved to read. She was lucky enough to live in a town that allowed girls to be schooled alongside the boys. It was not so everywhere. Just across the Connecticut River from Amherst, in Hatfield, Massachusetts, for example, a girl who wanted an education—like Sophia Smith (who later founded Smith College)—had to sit on the steps of the schoolhouse and listen to the boys inside.

While so far no concrete information exists on Emily's relationship as a young girl with Mrs. Mack, it seems likely that they saw each other often and that Mary Ely Mack—of all the adults in the household—would have had the time and energy to give the engaging and delightful young poet some attention.

This is what we know: The Macks bought the Dickinson house at a foreclosure auction in 1833 when Emily was three, so for her Mrs. Mack must have seemed part of the family by the time this book takes place. Emily's grandfather had lost a lot of money with bad investments, so the only way any of the Dickinsons could remain at the Homestead was for Grandfather Dickinson to sell the house. Then the younger Dickinson family was able to rent the east wing, which had once been their grandfather's roomy quarters. The Dickinsons lived in the east wing until Emily was nine, then moved away to another house in town. When David Mack died in 1854, Father Dickinson bought the house back. And that is where the adult Emily lived until her death.

Emily's father was by all accounts a distant man. When Emily was a grown woman, she once remarked about him that "my father only reads on Sundays—he reads lonely & rigorous books." Her mother was often ill, though she did a lot of the baking, which Emily liked to do as well. Mrs. Dickinson was known for her doughnuts, coconut cake, and custards. Emily also exchanged recipes with neighbors, friends, and relatives, and may have included some from Mrs. Mack in her repertoire.

Emily had a close relationship in those early days with her brother, Austin, a year and a half older, and with Lavinia, called Vinnie, almost three years younger. Eventually, though, her closest companion was her dog, Carlo, which her father had given her to take on her long walks in Amherst's fields and woods. Emily was an ardent gardener, too. Her father attached a greenhouse to the Homestead so that Emily could garden all year round.

The first part of this story is a reconstruction of Emily's early days, taking what we know about how Emily wrote—on all those chance slips of paper—and showing her doing the same thing as a small child. It was her grown-up niece, Martha Dickinson Bianchi, who dubbed them "chance slips." These pieces of found paper with her poems written on them can be seen at both Harvard University and Amherst College in their manuscript collections.

Emily's handwriting remained hard to read—and absolutely not straight! She erased and scribbled over bits of her poems as she revised them. Editors and scholars have long argued about many of the actual words in her poems, not to mention the punctuation!

I live twenty minutes from the Homestead, which is now a museum dedicated to Dickinson and her poetry. For visits to both the Homestead and the Evergreens, where Austin and his family lived—just a hedge away—see the museum website: emilydickinsonmuseum.org. You might even find me puttering around there. My favorite place is Emily's bedroom, where she composed a good number of her poems. Published poets are now allowed to write there for an hour. I have done it twice. I could feel her quiet presence by my side as I wrote in short lines in the waning light.

# Some Emily Dickinson Poems

There are a number of text references to Emily's poems in this book. Here are a few of them. Emily's poems were written when she was an adult, but it is easy to see how much nature figured into her work. She loved nature and the world around her from an early age. Most of Emily's poems have no titles unless given so by collection editors.

These poems are excerpted from three volumes:

1890 ***Poems by Emily Dickinson***
Edited by Mabel Loomis Todd and T. W. Higginson.
Published by Roberts Brothers of Boston.

1891 ***Poems by Emily Dickinson, Second Series***
Edited by T. W. Higginson and Mabel Loomis Todd.
Published by Roberts Brothers of Boston.

1896 ***Poems by Emily Dickinson, Third Series***
Edited by Mabel Loomis Todd.
Published by Roberts Brothers of Boston.

**I'm nobody! Who are you?**
**Are you nobody, too?**
**Then there's a pair of us – don't tell!**
**They'd banish us, you know.**

**How dreary to be somebody!**
**How public, like a frog**
**To tell your name the livelong day**
**To an admiring bog!**

These are only the first two verses of a much longer poem:

**There is a flower that bees prefer,**
**And butterflies desire;**
**To gain the purple democrat**
**The humming-birds aspire**

**And whatsoever insect pass,**
**A honey bears away**
**Proportioned to his several dearth**
**And her capacity.**

This is the first verse of a much longer poem:

**I have not told my garden yet,**
**Lest that should conquer me;**
**I have not quite the strength now**
**To break it to the bee.**

This one is written on an envelope and can be seen at the Amherst College website, acdc.amherst.edu/view/asc:16116:

**The way Hope builds his House**

**It is not with a sill –**
**Nor Rafter – has that Edifice**
**But only Pinnacle –**

**Abode in as supreme**
**This superficies**
**As if it were of Ledges smit**
**Or mortised with the Laws –**

# Bibliography


Gordon, Lyndall. *Lives Like Loaded Guns: Emily Dickinson and Her Family's Feuds*. New York: Penguin Group, 2010.

Grabher, Gudrun, Roland Hagenbüchle, and Cristanne Miller, eds. *The Emily Dickinson Handbook*. Amherst: University of Massachusetts Press, 1998.

Johnson, Thomas H., ed. *Emily Dickinson: Selected Letters*, 3 vols. Cambridge, MA: The Belknap Press of Harvard University Press, 1971.

Johnson, Thomas H., ed. *The Complete Poems of Emily Dickinson*. Boston: Little, Brown and Company, 1960.

Langton, Jane, and Nancy Ekholm Burkert. *Acts of Light: Emily Dickinson*. Boston: New York Graphic Society, 1980.

Liebling, Jerome, et al. *The Dickinsons of Amherst*. Hanover, NH: University Press of New England, 2001.

Longsworth, Polly. *The World of Emily Dickinson: A Visual Biography*. New York: W. W. Norton & Company, 1990.

National Endowment for the Arts. Reader Resources: *The Poetry of Emily Dickinson*. Washington, D.C., n.d.

Sewall, Richard B. *The Life of Emily Dickinson*. Reprint, Cambridge, MA: Harvard University Press, 1998.

Wolff, Cynthia Griffin. *Emily Dickinson*. New York: Alfred. A. Knopf, 1986.

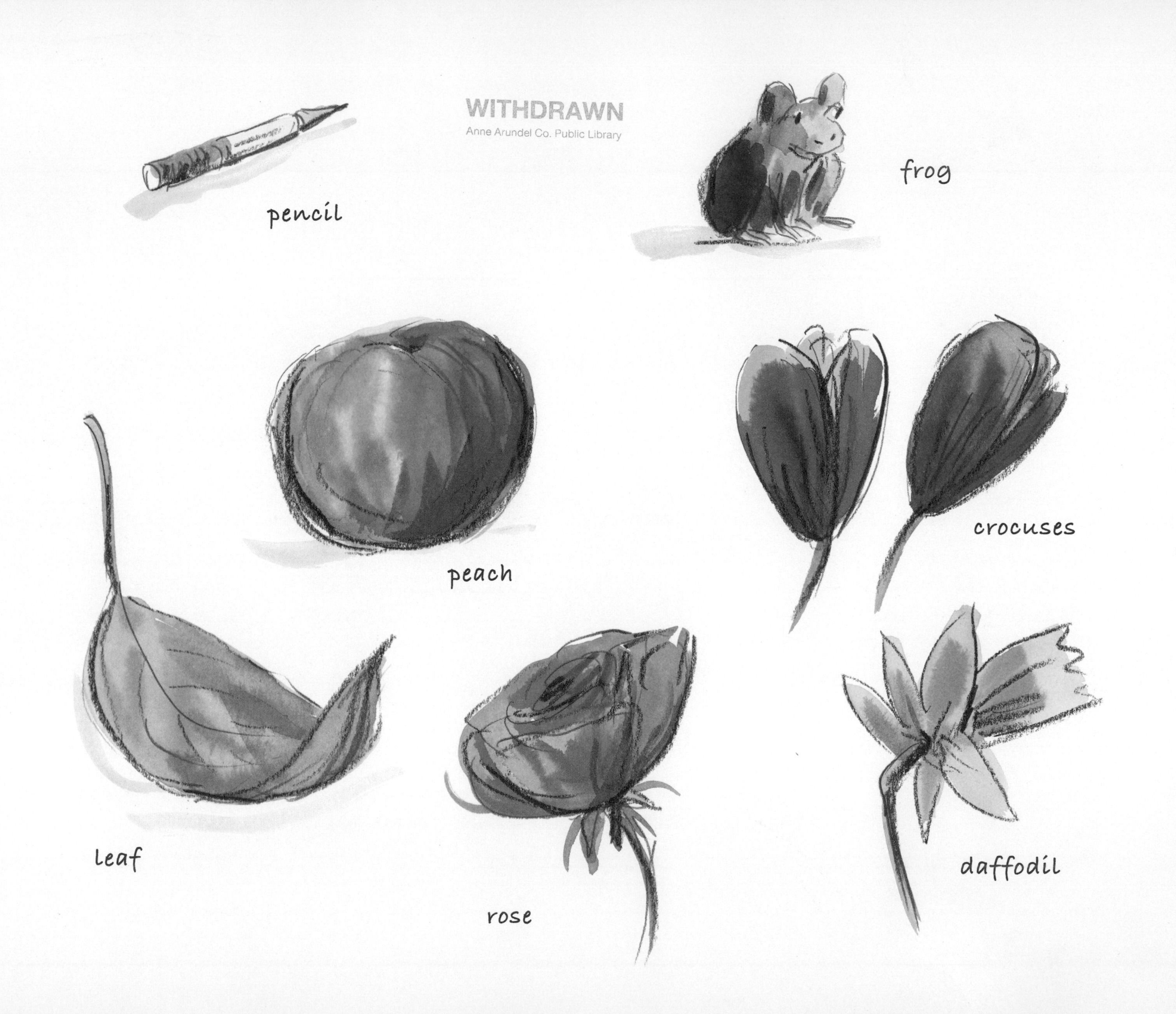
pencil
frog
peach
crocuses
leaf
rose
daffodil